BITTLE

By Patricia MacLachlan & Emily MacLachlan
Illustrations by Dan Yaccarino

JOANNA COTLER BOOKS
An Imprint of HarperCollinsPublishers

Bittle

Text copyright © 2004 by Patricia MacLachlan and Emily MacLachlan

Illustrations copyright © 2004 by Dan Yaccarino

Manufactured in China by South China Printing Company Ltd. All rights reserved.

www.harperchildrens.com

Library of Congress Cataloging-in-Publication Data

MacLachlan, Patricia.

  Bittle / by Patricia MacLachlan & Emily MacLachlan ; illustrations by Dan Yaccarino.—1st ed.

    p.   cm.

  Summary: Nigel the cat and Julia the dog think they will have no use for the new baby in their

house, but after a while they realize that they have come to love her.

    ISBN 0-06-000961-6 — ISBN 0-06-000962-4 (lib. bdg.)

    [1. Babies—Fiction. 2. Pets—Fiction. 3. Cats—Fiction. 4. Dogs—Fiction.] I. Yaccarino, Dan, ill.

II. Title.

PZ7.M2225Bi 2004

[E]—dc21

                                                                           2003002357

Typography by Alicia Mikles

1 2 3 4 5 6 7 8 9 10

❖

First Edition

For all the dogs and cats who have run our households:
Nigel
Hilly
Sarah
Tom
Kruk
Owen
Tess
Sylvie
Romeo
Emmet
Charlie
Bossi
Tanga
Wupsi
—P.M. AND E.M.

To Little Ben
—D.Y.

In a big yellow house lived a cat and a dog.

Nigel chased mice in the fields. When he could, he scratched the rugs.

Julia didn't care about mice or rug scratching. She cared about treats and bones and sleeping. Sometimes she slept fourteen hours a day.

They were happy.

But one day something new happened.

The woman who lived in the house brought home tiny clothes—socks and booties. Julia looked at them.

"They are not for me," she told Nigel.

The man painted a small room pale green.
"The color of mold," said Nigel.

The man moved a big piece of furniture into the room.
Julia sniffed it. "It's a cage."
Nigel rubbed against it.
"It's a crib," he said. "It's for a baby."

"A baby!" said Julia. "We don't need a baby!"
"I think we're getting one," said Nigel. He stretched and scratched the rug under the crib.

On a windy day the baby was born. She came home wrapped
in a pink blanket. The baby had dark eyes and no hair.

Julia smelled her. "That doesn't smell like anything I know,"
she said. "What good is she? She's just a little bit of a thing."

"Bittle!" Nigel said happily. "That's what we'll call her."

But Julia was not happy. She was worried.

She moved her bones, one by one by one, to a new hiding place.

"They're my bones. Bittle will want them," Julia told Nigel.

"She has no teeth," said Nigel. "Not yet."

The man and woman thought Bittle slept all night long. But she didn't.

"Waaaaah," cried Bittle.

Nigel and Julia ran to her crib.
Julia barked. "Stop that! That's a bad sound!"

But Bittle cried harder. Nigel jumped into the crib. He curled up next to Bittle and purred. She stopped crying.

Some nights Bittle was wide-awake. She wanted company.
Nigel batted the mobile above Bittle's bed.
He sang her a song.

"Meow at the stars,
    howl at the moon.
Sleep, little Bittle,
    the sun will rise soon."

Nigel meowed. He tried to howl.

"That's not a howl, that's a yowl," said Julia.

"Here's how you howl."

"**Whoooooooooo,**" howled Julia.

Bittle liked it. Bittle smiled.

Sometimes Bittle threw toys out of the crib.

Bear

Bunny

Horse

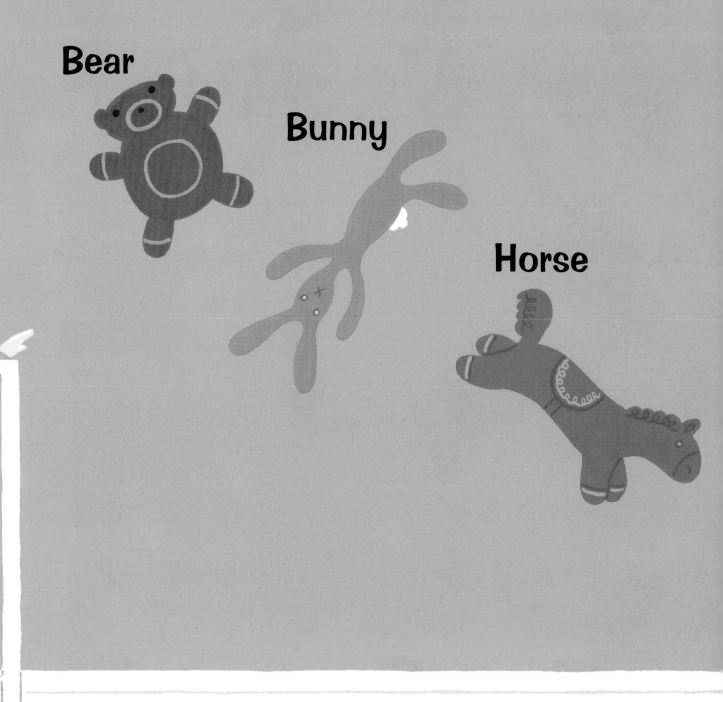

Doll

Rattle

Ball

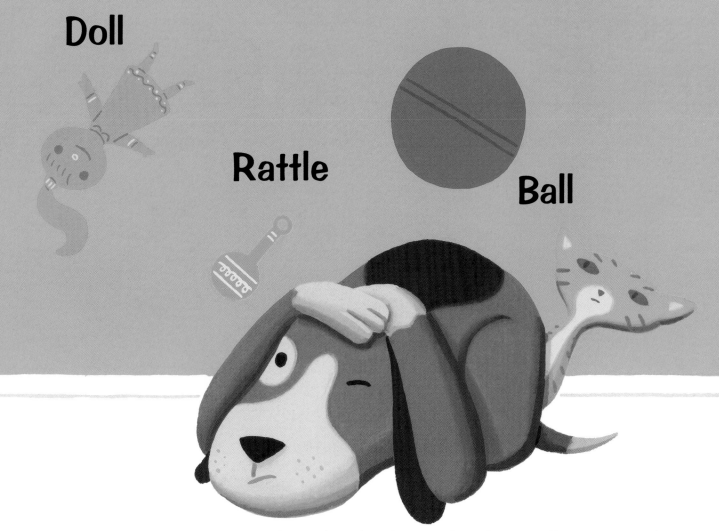

Nigel and Julia brought them all back to her.

Except for one.

Sometimes Nigel and Julia watched Bittle until she fell asleep.

"This is hard work," said Nigel. He closed his eyes.

"But sometimes it's fun," said Julia.

Nigel opened one eye and looked at Julia, surprised.
"Sometimes," said Julia.
And they curled up underneath the crib and slept.

When Bittle began to crawl, she was lightning fast.
Nigel and Julia followed her in and out of the house.

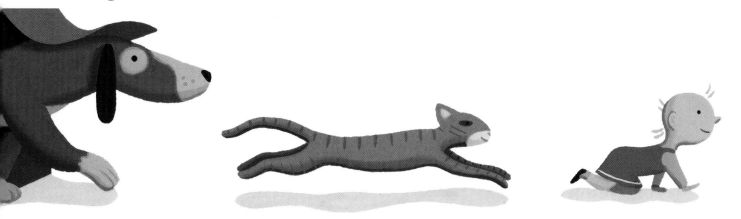

Bittle liked the daisies in the garden.
She tried to catch butterflies.
"I like butterflies, too," said Nigel. "We are a lot alike."

Bittle liked the toilet in the bathroom.

"I love that toilet," said Julia. "Bittle and I are alike, too."

When Bittle got tired, she slept with Nigel and Julia in a heap in the sun, her head under Julia's chin.

At breakfast Bittle threw her biscuits to Julia.
She dropped pieces of scrambled egg to Nigel.
"I like Bittle," said Nigel. "She shares."

"I like her too," said Julia. She licked
cinnamon oatmeal off of Bittle's foot.
"In fact, I love her," said Julia.

Just then Bittle spoke for the very first time.
"She's trying to say a word!" said the woman.

"Say 'mama'!"

"Woof,"
said Bittle.

"Say 'papa'!"
said the man.

"Meow,"
said Bittle.

And then Bittle did something that surprised them all.

It was not barking. It was not meowing.

It was something that Nigel, Julia, and Bittle could all do together.

"Whooooooooo!"